Is Daddy Really Dead?

by E.L. Hutton

DORRANCE
PUBLISHING CO
EST. 1920
PITTSBURGH, PENNSYLVANIA 15238

Dorrance Publishing Co
585 Alpha Drive
Pittsburgh, PA 15238
Visit our website at www.dorrancebookstore.com

ISBN: 978-1-6366-1290-4
eISBN: 978-1-6366-1876-0

Preface

Life and change can arrive without a moment's notice. This is when we discover that we have the strength to go on, even when we feel that life has taken our dreams, and all control out of our life.

It is at this point that from someplace deep within, we discover that there is something inside of us that is not just a voice in our head; but something deep inside of us that compels us to keep moving forward. This is God's gift to many who have experienced sudden and drastic changes in their life that they never planned on.

Chapter 1

A Dark Morning

A loud crack of thunder and chain lightning flashes across the sky, and a light rain begins to fall. A long, black limousine pulls into the cemetery. It parks, and Elaine Williams steps out and is greeted by an usher who walks her to a white tent where many people are taking their seats. This is where her husband's casket is covered with flowers in preparation for his ceremony of "Goodbye."

This cemetery is quite lovely with large trees, well-kept grass, and areas with benches for those who visit the deceased. The choice made for this cemetery was, of course, decided by Robert's parents. Elaine approves but is very unhappy that she was not allowed to make any decisions for her husband.

The fact is all details were taken care of before she even had a chance to think about it. Robert has been dead only three days, and everything was quickly taken care of without any conversation with Elaine. He was her husband, and it was as if she did not even exist!

Elaine is guided to a seat at the front closest to Robert's casket, which is covered with flowers in preparation for the ceremony. Elaine takes her seat and adjusts her dark glasses to hide her tears as she sits next to her two daughters.

Mandy is eleven years old and Lizzy is six. They smile and give their mom a hug. She motions to them to take their seats. The children are not sure what all of this means. They just know this is something serious but not sure why they are there. Ellen believes that they do not really realize that their Daddy is gone and not coming back.

Mandy knows her dad has died but does not seem to accept that he is gone forever. Lizzy is not sure why they are there or what all this really means. They have never had anyone die in their lives.

1

Lizzy leans over and asks her Mom, "Why are so many people here? Are we going to have a party?"

Elaine smiles and quietly says, "In a way. They are all here because they love your daddy and want to make sure he knows it." Elaine's voice breaks, and she sends Lizzy back to her seat. She nods at Janet to take care of the girls, so they stay seated.

Janet is the stepmom to Robert and Patrick is his father. The family is all seated together with her mother, Barbara, seated at the end of the row next to Patrick. The children are sitting in between Elaine and Janet so they can keep the girls seated and quiet.

The pastor walks to the casket and begins his sermon. Thankfully, the rain has lifted and there is just a slight breeze. Hopefully, the ceremony can go by quickly as this is the last place that Elaine wants to be.

Elaine has advised the Pastor that she is the one in control of this ceremony not Robert's parents. The Pastor acknowledges and honors her wishes with nothing being said to Robert's parents.

Lizzy leans over to her Mom and says, "Mommy, why is everyone so sad? What is wrong?"

Elaine puts her finger to her lips and whispers, "We must be quiet now." Mandy grabs her sister's hand.

The Sermon begins, the Pastor acknowledges everyone, and begins with a prayer. After about fifteen minutes into the sermon, Elaine cannot take any more of the sadness.

She becomes very impatient with this whole thing and she just cannot listen anymore. She whispers to herself, "This is wrong, all wrong. I know he is not dead; I just know it!" She slides her dark glasses down on her nose and motions to the minister to wrap up the sermon.

The minister gets the message, raises his eyebrows and begins to end with, "Robert will be missed by all and never forgotten. May he rest in peace." He slowly, steps away from the casket.

Elaine stands up and everyone follows. There are murmurs throughout the guests asking each other: "Why so short? We didn't get to pay our respects."

Elaine turns as Janet's voice comes over the microphone telling all to be sure to come by their house for a reception with food and drink.

Janet walks over to Elaine and grabs the two girls' hands and tells her she will take them back to their house; Elaine nods in agreement. She tells Janet that she needs a few moments alone.

Janet nods with approval and walks to the parking lot with the girls. When she puts the girls in the back seat of the limo, she shakes her head and tells the girl's. "Sometimes I just don't understand your Mom." She advises the limo driver that it will be a few minutes before they will be ready to leave.

Patrick gets out of the car and goes around to Janet and gives her a hug. She smiles at him.

"How nice of you. I needed that."

By the time Janet goes around to the other side to get in the car, Lizzy has jumped out and is running across the lawn toward her mother.

Janet gets out of the car and Mandy tells her not to worry, that she will be okay. Janet frowns and stands next to the car watching Mandy, as she runs to her mom.

Elaine kneels at the casket with her head bowed and her hands on the casket. "Robert, Robert are you there? I can't believe you are dead. I just know that somehow you did not die. Please help me find you." She bows her head and begins to sob.

The cemetery is clearing out as Lizzy comes skipping up to the casket. "Mommy, don't cry, don't be sad. Daddy, is coming home!"

Elaine, hugs her and says, "Honey, why do you say that?"

"He told me so! He said don't worry I will be home soon."

Elaine grabs Lizzy's hand and they walk back to the parking lot. Lizzy is so carefree, skipping along and talking a mile a minute.

"Lizzy, did you dream about Daddy last night?"

"No, not in my sleep. Daddy, came to my room and told me to not worry, that he would be home soon!" She gives her Mom a big smile.

"Lizzy, did he touch you, hug you, or sit on the bed with you?"

"No, Mommy, he just stood at the end of my bed and told me not to worry."

Elaine shakes her head and tells herself that just as she thought, there is more to this whole thing than anyone knows. They arrive back at the car and Janet jumps out and puts Lizzy into the back seat of the limo and turns to Elaine with a frown on her face. "We have got to hurry; you don't want to be late. People will be arriving soon." She shakes her finger at Elaine. "You show up and do the proper thing!"

Elaine turns and walks away with a wave of her hand. She yells back at Janet, "I'll come in a bit, I have to do something."

Chapter 2

Days Gone Bye

 *Transported Back in Time:*

Elaine walks over to her little sports car that she strategically parked in the parking lot earlier. She knew that she would need to be alone after the funeral. She drives to her favorite park that has big trees and water running in a small brook. It always gives her peace to be here.

A large tree is shading the perfect spot to park. She parks the car and rolls down her window. She takes a deep breath of the breeze gently blowing in and tilts her head back on the seat and listens to the water running in the brook. She closes her eyes and is transported back to the morning when Robert told her he was going away for a few days.

As the breeze floats across her face, her eyes get heavy and she falls into a deep sleep. She goes back to the days before her husband died and things were all so natural and happy.

She and Robert had a wonderful marriage and two lovely children. Robert worked with determination to become more than a district manager for the corporation he worked for. His hope was to work his way to a position of VP or above.

Chapter 3

A Week Earlier

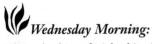***Wednesday Morning:***
Elaine had just finished in the bathroom and comes out in her nightgown with a smile on her face. Robert was standing there, as if he was waiting for her. Still in his pajama bottoms, he slips his arms around her.

"You know how much I love you, don't you?"

"Ah... oh, what are you up to? Of course, I know how much you mean to me. You do know you mean everything to me, don't you?"

Dancing in a circle with her, he whispers, "Together we must always be together; it is destined."

"You all right? What are you up to?"

Robert smiles like an impish kid. "I want to do something I haven't done in a long time."

Elaine smiles and starts to drop her nightgown, and he laughs and says, "No, no, that will come later."

Elaine pulls her nightgown back on her shoulders and makes a funny face at him.

He smiles and says, "I want to go up and see my grandmother!"

Elaine smiles, "That sounds like fun. The kids would love that."

Robert shakes his head. "Not this time. I must go alone. I want to spend some time with her. I have questions from my childhood that I want to her ask her about. I just feel like I need to do this on my own. We will go another time as a family."

Elaine steps back from him with a frown and then a smile.

"Do you have a girlfriend that looks a lot like your grandmother?"

"No way! I'll be back on Sunday early evening for sure."

"It seems that this is something that you really need to do, so go." She gives him a nod of approval and a smile as she begins to straighten the sheets on the bed.

Robert's face turns serious. "I just need to check into a few things that have been bothering me about my grandparents. My father is the last person I want to go to. He has never been the father to me that I should have had. I need to figure some things out for myself. When I am done and find out what I need to know, you and I will have a long talk about all of it. I promise."

Elaine can tell how important this is to him, so she does not dispute it with him.

"Okay. Well, I will be very glad to see you and to find out what the mystery is all about. I'll wait and see, but only because I Love you."

Robert gets dressed quickly and tells her he can't be late and today is a big day. "Thanks, baby, you are the best!"

He quickly leaves the bedroom and almost runs down the stairs. She can see how happy he is that she did not give him any problems with his quest.

Elaine heads to the kitchen to feed and take care of the kids. Robert is already there hugging the kids and telling them to have a great day! He gives her his million-dollar smile, waves, and says, "See you later."

She watches him go out the front door as he turns with a smile and a wave. She cannot help but smile. She is so eager to be with him when he gets home in the evening. She decides to make a great dinner and put the kids to bed early. So, they can have some quality time. Elaine turns to the kids with a smile and motions for them to come on.

"Chop, chop. Let's go! Get your things. We don't want to be late for school." The kids run upstairs to get their bags. The trip to school is easy, the kids seem happy and so does she. She waves goodbye to the kids and drives off.

"Hmmm, all by myself; think I'll call Mom and see if she wants to do a bit of shopping and have lunch." Her mom answers the phone on the first ring! "Mom, were you expecting a call?" Her mom tells her that she was hoping it was her and that she was feeling lonely.

Elaine smiles to herself and heads directly to her mom's house, knowing that she must keep busy so she can stop all the thoughts running through her head about whatever Robert is up to.

As she turns up her mom's block, the sky suddenly turns gray and it begins to drizzle rain. She honks her horn for her mom to come out. A minute later, her mom comes running toward the car to avoid getting too wet. She has a big smile on her face.

"Hi, honey. So glad you called. I wondered what I was going to do today."

Elaine shifts her thinking and smiles at her mom. "Yeah, let's go have some fun. Mom, I'm really happy we can be together today!"

Chapter 4

The Luncheon

 Wednesday:

Robert is meeting his father for lunch so he can ask his dad about what happened that caused him to stop him from seeing his grandparents.

Robert walks in the door and see's that Patrick has already arrived. Patrick, of course, is there early enjoying his second cocktail. This is one of his dad's favorite Italian restaurants. If you are going to have a meal with Dad, this always seemed to be his choice. Robert greets his dad with a hug and takes his seat.

"Good God, Robert, you look wonderful! The world's been treating you right, I take it?"

"Well, Dad, I can't complain, just working long hours, but as you say, hard work is what pays off in the long run."

"Got that right!" Patrick raises his glass and smiles.

"Father, something has been on my mind for a while, and you are probably the only one who can solve the puzzle I have going on in my mind."

Patrick furls his eyebrows and says, "That sounds serious."

"Dad, do you remember when Grandfather died?"

"Of, course I do."

"I was about twelve years old."

Patrick corrects him. "I think you just had your eleventh birthday. Why are you asking?"

"Well, Dad, when he died, I was old enough to be going to Grandfather's funeral. I remember you and Janet went, but never said a word to me, until after the funeral. It made me incredibly sad to not have gone to

Grandfather's funeral. I would have very much liked to say goodbye like everyone else. It bothers me that you let me spend most of my free time with Grandfather, but never even told me about his death, the funeral, or anything until it was over. Why didn't you tell me and let me go to the funeral? It eats at me that he just disappeared out of my life. You have no idea how much that hurt me."

Robert watches as Patrick becomes uncomfortable and squirms in his chair and loosens his tie. "What is wrong with you? Is this difficult for you to talk about?"

Patrick becomes stressed and begins to turn pale. He looks down at the table and says, "Well, I just thought it was better for you to not have to be involved in all the grieving."

As Robert leans forward to say something more to his dad, the waiter arrives with their orders and refreshes their wine. Patrick fidgets in his chair and takes a large gulp of his scotch, finishing it off. "You were just a young boy and probably don't remember too much about your grandfather." That was the wrong thing to say to Robert.

Robert stares coldly at his father, and it takes everything he has not to yell at him. "You sent me to my grandfather's whenever I was not in school from the time, I was four or five years old and, if I remember right, I celebrated all my birthdays with him! He would make it a big event and I loved him for it! How could you be so cold? Did you ever think of how I might feel? Saying goodbye to him would have helped me a lot. You are truly unbelievable!"

"Hold on right there. I thought I was saving you from the grief of knowing your grandfather had died when you were such a young age. I didn't want you to experience that."

"After that you started telling me that I needed to stay home with you and Janet and become more responsible and that play was over. It was not until I was out of junior high when you told me the reason you never sent me back was that Grandma was ill and that Grandfather didn't have time for me. Now I realize that that was all a lie. I want the truth of why you stopped my relationship with my grandparents!"

"All that time you let me believe something about my grandparents that was not true! Did you ever give a thought to how much that affected me? You have never been a good father to me. I always wanted to look up to you until

I grew up and I started to see the real man you were. Boy, oh boy, I was so stupid to believe everything or anything you ever told me! I really, thought that Grandfather for some reason no longer cared about me."

"All right, Robert, don't get so uptight! What can I do for you?"

Patrick's mind was racing, he knew he had to end this and get to the bottom of what Robert was saying and stop all the questions.

Robert leans back in his chair staring at his dad and quietly says, "Father, what happened to Grandfather's estate? I never heard anything about it?"

Patrick decides to not rebut Robert and talks in a low voice. "It went to probate, I presume. He had his attorney friend handle everything."

"Didn't they have a reading of the will?"

Patrick looks has his watch, "Ah oh…," he mumbles as he starts getting up out of his chair. "Got to go, I'm late!" He gets up and grabs his coat, and some papers fall out of his inside pocket. He quickly grabs the papers and heads for the entrance of the restaurant. He turns and with a quick wave, walks out the front door. He never gave Robert a chance to say goodbye.

The waiter brings the bill and picks up a piece of paper on the floor, and shows it to Robert, "Is this yours?"

Robert says, "No, oh, wait a minute, I believe that is mine." He takes the envelope and sees that it is addressed to "Master Robert Williams." He furrows his brow, wondering why his name is on an envelope that his father had tucked into his jacket.

With a second look, he sees that the date on the envelope was from several years ago. Now mumbling to himself he says, "Why I would have been about twelve years old when this was written! Why, was this letter kept from me? What is he hiding from me?"

Robert now is more determined than ever to find out the truth about his grandfather's Will. Robert returns to his house and heads up the stairs to his private office, calling down the stairs in case someone is home, "Will be busy for a couple of hours." A warning just in case anyone was home.

As he sits down in his chair, he calls Steve, a childhood friend who was almost like a brother to him, as they spent many years of their young lives playing together.

Robert's dad kindly welcomed Steve into the family. As a young boy, Steve was really left on his own with no one that seemed to care about him. So, we could say the good side of Patrick was that he had the heart to rescue Steve. As Steve and Robert grew older and as, teenagers they seemed to go their separate ways.

Steve, after several years as a young man had some rough years and was rescued by Robert's father who gave him work and fill-in jobs just to keep Steve afloat. Robert really had not seen Steve in many years and was not sure what he was presently doing with his life.

Robert impatiently taps his fingers on the desk while he waits for Steve to answer the phone. When Steve picks up, Robert, greets him feeling quite awkward and stumbles with his words.

"Long time to hear or see you; this is Robert. Remember me?"

Steve laughs and says, "Of course I do. You been drinking or something? Your words are all messed up!"

Robert laughs and says, "Didn't know how you would feel about me calling you. You know I still think of you as a brother."

Steve says, "Right on, me too. I'm always here for you if you need me."

Robert jumps into the conversation about the weekend trip he wants to take up to Wisconsin to check out some information he is looking for.

"Steve, are you up for a day or two of playing detective. "I'm on a quest that will take us on a great trip over the weekend."

"Okay, any chance we might wind up in jail?"

Robert laughs. "Not that kind of a job. I want to search for some info in order to get some answers I need. I will tell you more once we meet and go over all the details. I will need a couple of more people to help as I have only a short time to do this. I will need to return home on Sunday."

Steve says he has a few guys who would be good and could help. Robert gives a thumb-up on that idea but mentions they would only need two more people, and he was thinking that since both knew Mike, maybe they could get him and one other person.

"Look, Steve, this is important that what we are doing does not get out to anyone."

"Sure thing."

"I would only ask people I could trust. This means a lot to me."

Steve nods. "Sure."

"I will tell you the plan when I see you."

Steve does not let Robert know that his boss, at the time, is Robert's father. He says, "I'm in, and should have no problem getting that time off."

Robert calls his friend Mike, and he is available, and he will join the group. Steve had said he would bring his friend Fred to be a part of this investigative group. Fred has also worked for Robert's father on odd jobs that no one really knows about. Fred is a stunt car driver on the side and does many other types of jobs for Patrick. Robert plans on the guys prowling around and gathering as much information as possible that can explain his grandfather's death and estate.

The plan is set for Steve to meet Robert at the end of town at an old, abandoned motel that has been deserted for many years. It is agreed that they will all meet and park behind the motel. Why it was never taken down, no one knows. Some people say it is haunted and no one wants to go there to tear it down. Probably, afraid they will let ghosts loose in the town.

It is agreed by all that this trip is not to be told to anyone at this time. They will go together in one vehicle. The only trip-up for Steve is he has always made himself available to Patrick for anything he wanted. He usually lets him know if for any reason he may not be available.

Steve calls Robert's father in order to stay in good graces with him. Steve lets him know that he will be out of town with his son for a weekend guy thing.

Not realizing that he may have made an error. He says to himself, *Hope I just didn't make a mistake.*

Patrick replies, "Should be fine. I'll get back to you."

Steve says to himself, *He better not get back to me. I'll be gone. I won't let Robert down.*

Chapter 5

The Truth Be Known

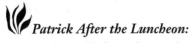*Patrick After the Luncheon:*

Patrick slams the front door as he comes in and heads for the living room and straight to the bar and pours himself a Bourbon. He collapses onto the sofa and sits with his head in his hands. Janet, Patrick's wife of many years, hears the door slam. She heads to the downstairs and sees Patrick in the living room and stops in her tracks.

"What in the world is the matter with you? You look like the world has fallen on your shoulders!" Lifting his face out of his hands and tries not to show his frustration, however, it does not work.

"It might as well have. My whole world may just fall apart. We may have big trouble if I am not careful."

Janet leans forward with panic in her voice. "What has happened?"

"I'll tell you. I think we have a major problem. I had lunch with Robert, or perhaps you could call it an inquisition. He was asking me, out of the blue, all these questions about his grandfather and why he was not told about the funeral. I personally will blame that on you."

Janet glares at him. "And I caused you to do what?"

Patrick shakes his head and puts his hand up, indicating he does not want to get into an argument. "I should have done things differently!"

Janet moves to the nearest chair and sits down and begins to just stare at him. She feels the color leave her face as she begins to think the worst. "What is going on?"

Patrick stares at her in wonderment of what he has just done. His eyes show disappointment and sadness at the mistake he just made. "I don't understand why he now has questions as a grown man about his grandfather?" He takes a sip of his drink and leans forward toward Janet and in a softer voice tells her, "I know you don't want to hear this, but I think he has probably found out something that has caused him to question everything about his grandfather's death."

Janet leans forward, more interested. She speaks almost in a whisper, as if someone might be listening. "Do you really think he is onto the truth about his grandfather's death?"

Patrick walks over to the bar and refreshes his drink. He hesitates as he looks at Janet, trying to evaluate her reaction to what he is about to tell her.

"I don't really know that he knows anything about his grandfather's death, but he sure is questioning the Will. He wants to know how his grandfather died and why we never spoke to him about it."

"My God, what he thinks he knows or doesn't know, is unimaginable." Janet looks down at the floor and then over to Patrick.

Patrick tells her, "I thought we made sure that this would never come up?"

Janet sits back in her chair and whispers, "So did I." Janet stands up debating whether to stay in this conversation or not. "Patrick, you did take care that the will would never be found, didn't you?"

"I had the will in my coat and was on my way to put it in the safe deposit box, so no one could get to it. My biggest mistake was to not go to the bank first before I met with Robert. We made plans and I did not want to be late."

"I met Robert for lunch and when I left, the papers fell out of my coat onto the floor. I grabbed them before anyone could see them. The envelope was missing when I took them to the deposit box. To top things off, I got a call from Steve, saying he would be gone with Robert for a guy's weekend!" Robert shakes his head and gulps the last of his drink. "A guy's weekend! They have not seen each other for years! Why is all of this is happening now? This will ruin everything if Robert ever finds out the truth!"

Janet, trying to be calm and logical, reminds him that Steve and Robert grew up together and had known each other most of their lives. "Patrick, maybe they just wanted to see each other again and nothing more. I think you are panicking too quickly."

"Janet, Steve hasn't spent any time with Robert in several years, don't believe they have even talked. That is what concerns me. No reason for them suddenly, out of the blue, to want to visit each other. There is definitely, a reason."

Feeling she needs one now, Janet walks over and pours herself a drink as she never expected this kind of a mess.

"Well, you know any conflict, regarding that will could mess up our life completely."

Whatever is going on, we must put a stop to it! As quietly, and confidentially as we can. You must stay calm and not panic. Just call Steve and fish a bit for what is going on."

Patrick nods. "I'll leave Steve a message to call me and to tell no one he is calling me. I hope I can catch him before they leave town."

Janet leaves the room and Patrick goes to his office and closes the door and calls Steve. There's no answer, so he leaves a message: "Dammit! Steve, call me before you go on this trip. I need to talk to you now, most important!"

Patrick gets his called around 9:00 p.m. Patrick is in his office with feet up on his desk smoking a cigar. Steve's voice is a bit agitated.

"What's up? What do you need? You know I'm leaving town."

"Exactly, that is why I'm calling. You are leaving town with Robert; that is so unusual. You guys haven't seen each other in a long time. Why now?"

"I've been thinking about him a lot lately, not sure why. So, when he called, I just decided to take him up on it." Patrick is silent. "Look, I'm just taking a little weekend vacation and meeting up with your son. What's so bad about that? Is there a problem?"

Patrick in a low voice says, "If it happens that there is anything unusual about this trip, you need to let me know. I want to see you as soon as you get back. I think that there might be some trouble brewing that I need to be ahead of. This is not the guys meeting for a weekend party."

"Okay, okay, relax. I've never let you down before." Steve hangs up the phone and under his breath, talking to himself, he says, "Man, hope I'm not getting into something that's going to bury me."

Patrick sits in his office telling himself, "You've got to get a handle on this." He nods and picks up the phone. *I'll give Fred a call and use him for my backup.*

It rings and there is an answer: "Hey?"

"Fred, is that you?"

"Yeah, what's up?" Fred has done a lot of small jobs for Patrick. He is not tied to him. He just tolerates him. Fred figures Patrick feels the same about him.

19

"What's up? I need your help on a weekend project."

Patrick tells him that he wants him to call Steve and see if he wants to hang out for the weekend? "If he suggests you do something with him that he has planned, agree and then call me. I will explain. Steve must never know we have talked, got it?"

Fred agrees. "You know this is goanna cost you; the bigger the deal the bigger the cost."

"You're not questioning what I pay you are you?"

"No, man, it's all good."

"You've made a ton of money off me. Don't let me down. I'll wait for your callback tonight."

Fred agrees and reassures him that he has got nothing to worry about.

Patrick goes back to the living room and grabs a drink for himself and Janet. He heads upstairs and notices the door at the stairway to the attic is ajar. He goes up to the door to see why it is open and there sits Janet on the floor with papers spread out on the carpet.

"Janet, what in the world are you doing?"

"I thought I'd better take a look at this old stuff and make sure we don't have any letters, or anything lying around that could confirm what we have done."

Patrick walks over and pulls her up to her feet. "You are worrying? That's just not you."

Janet looks down at everything she has spread out on the floor and then back at Patrick. "Well, I know, but since all of this has come up, I thought I should make sure there is nothing else that belongs in our box at the bank. Are you sure no one else can get into that box?"

"Absolutely, that is no problem. The only thing that could happen would be for you and me to die and then my attorney knows that is the only time that he would have access. He knows what he has to do."

Let's pick all of this up and get out of here." Janet stuffs what she has found back in the box, with every intention to double-check when Patrick is not in the house, just to satisfy her own mind.

As they walk to their bedroom, he puts his arm around Janet and tells, her, "Don't worry, everything will be okay."

She nods and smiles. "Let's go to bed."

Chapter 6

Friday Morning Trip

*A Foggy Morning:*

As if the abandoned motel is not bad enough. It is an eerie place and as far as Roberts is concerned it probably does have ghosts. The fog rolls in, adding to the eerie feeling. Steve pulls his car around and parks in the back of the old motel, where he is to meet Robert. Robert has already arrived and has parked his car. Yet, the car is empty, and Robert is nowhere in sight. There is a rustling of the bushes just beyond where the cars are parked. Steve quickly turns and grabs his gun from under the seat! Out of the mist comes Robert zipping up his pants.

"Jesus, Steve. You gonna shoot me?"

"You ass! Scared the hell out of me."

Robert laughs. "I forgot that you pack, or I'd have been a little careful."

"Where are the other guys?"

Just then the other two guys pull up and park their cars. Robert opens his car doors and motions for everyone to get in. He brought his black Pathfinder with a gold license plate. The guys kid him about the plate. He tells them it reminds him that there is gold out there for him.

Steve says, "Yeah, sure thing. Let me know when you find it."

Robert explains the importance of the will and that it is for his information only. He gives the guys a scenario of what he wants and locations that they will be searching. He gives each of them a sheet with what they will be doing and looking for.

"Look, you guys, much of what we want is probably in the attorney's office or storage. You will have to look for an office in the house basement of my grandfather's attorney. He handled everything for my grandfather. Only problem is that he is now dead as well!"

Fred and Steve agree to work together searching the office and house. Mike is to check out the libraries, newspapers, and any other written information that he can find. Mike is a natural for making notes and organizing any paperwork they find.

Robert lets Mike know that he is an important key for him. "Just be sure you get as much info written in public records and anything else you can think of that will be good backup for me." They shake hands in agreement.

Chapter 7

Plan in Action

Robert explains that he will meet with his grandmother and get all the info he can, and if anything comes up, he will call them on their phones.

"What I do know is that attorney and his wife had two homes. One an office and the other was their home. By what I discovered just looking up attorneys in this area, it seems most were in town close enough to be able to walk to the courthouse. I will talk to my grandmother and then phone you with any info that might help you. Once I call you with the addresses, then get busy, as we don't want to run out of time. I will be meeting with my grandmother for breakfast early at 8:00 a.m.

"It may be that the houses that attorney used were never cleared out after his death.

If it is possible, we might check if there were any relatives who knew he had died. In case we do not find anything missing, perhaps we can contact a still-living relative. We will have to talk that over before we take any action. So, we will have to do some searching without alerting anyone. I think the house that he worked in is still the way it was before he died and possibly still has all his papers there as well. Just gather what's there and bring it to me.

"You will know exactly where you are going and what you will need to do, including what precautions to take. We must be sure that we leave no evidence that anyone has been there. I will talk to my grandmother and find out everything I can. See if you can hit maybe the library and see if you can't look up any news or papers that may have had anything covering my grandfather's will."

He shows them the envelope with the date and tells them to really search around the date, as he thinks it may be very close to the time his grandfather may have known his life was coming to an end.

"Hopefully, we will find a death certificate, will, or something that will help me answer my questions. Jeez, I don't really know. Just find me everything and anything that would help. No extra TVs or large things that we have to haul. In other words, don't just decide to take back a whole file cabinet, just for an easier way of searching!" He laughs and the guys chime in with "you must think we're crazy or something." Everyone laughs.

Chapter 8

Saturday Morning

Saturday morning, Robert meets with his grandmother while the guys are fielding the information that they found at the newspaper office and the library on Friday afternoon.

At 6:00 p.m. just as the sun was going down, Steve and Mike head to attorney's house.

"Yep, looks like it's been vacant for a while, except that it is still furnished and looks like they never really vacated this place."

They are looking in the windows and trying the door when a woman from across the street walks up to them on the porch. Both guys jump and turn.

Steve quickly asks, "Is the owner or his relatives here by chance? We are trying to locate them. Wanted to talk to Paul if we could. We are friends of his son, who asked us to drop by."

"Why no, he passed away, quite a while ago. No one ever came to clean out the houses. There were two of them. One for the office and one they lived in. You know he was quite a loner and had a lovely wife, but she never really stayed here. You know Paul was an attorney and did a lot of his work from this house."

"Well, what about his wife, could we talk to her?"

"No, she died. I think he was quite lost without her." She points to the upstairs window of the house. "He seemed to spend a lot of time at the office. Maybe he was terribly busy, however, it didn't seem that way. I think he may have missed his wife more than he thought he would. He was always nice, never acted broken up, always very polite."

"That's too bad," Steve replied. Steve did not want to look at her, as it did kind of get to him. He knew what it was like to feel all alone. He shook her hand and thanked her for all her help. He turned with a wave of his hand and headed back to where they had parked the car. When they reached the car, he checked to see if anyone was watching them.

"I sure hope that old lady doesn't go talking to the neighbors about seeing us." They get into the car and turn on the first street they can find to leave the neighborhood from a different street.

Fred glances at Steve. "Are you paranoid?"

Steve says, "Hell no; just don't want a problem."

Chapter 9

Renewal of Hearts

Saturday morning, Robert shows up at his grandmother's house with a bouquet of flowers. He knocks on the door and his grandmother quickly opens the door and begins to cry.

"Come in, I wish your grandfather were here; he would be so happy to see you."

Robert hugs her and says, "I wish Grandfather were here too. I never once stopped wanting to be with you and Grandfather. I love you very much." They hugged and cried together. She gives him a big hug and wipes a tear away with her apron.

"Grandma you are just like I remember you; doesn't seem like you've aged at all, just a little different hair color." She smiles and hugs him again.

"I've been waiting so long to see you. You are so grown-up, a man, a real man. Robert, oh Robert, why did you stay away so long? Your grandfather and I missed you so. Why did you just stop coming or calling?" Robert looks horrified.

"Grandma, Dad, told me that you guys felt I should be with them and not come to see you anymore. He told me you were ill, and Grandfather did not have time for me anymore."

"Oh, my goodness, no. Your dad told us you were growing up and too busy for adults and that he would try to get you to come for a visit and that never happened."

"Grandmother, as long as I live, I will always be here for you. I will leave you all my numbers, phone, and address so that you can always get in touch with me. And I need all the help you can give me. I want to find out what happened to Grandfather's will. Do you have a copy?"

She pours him a cup of coffee and sits down with him. Placing a dish of fruit and some rolls on the table.

"I don't have a copy of his will. Your grandfather took care of all the business parts of our life. I know his intention was that you would be in the will, as he wanted you to know how much we cared. We had even put away enough money to pay for your education, wedding and put some money away for future children."

"I never knew of any of this. I am trying right now to figure out what the truth was. Do you know what Grandfather did with all the paperwork?"

"Well, yes I believe it would be with his friend who was an attorney. Paul Sanders, Attorney at Law; his office was downtown on Third and Elm Street."

"He died about two years ago. You know, he lived the last years of his life in the upstairs part of his office on Elm Street, said it was easier than getting a ride to the office. He did love his work. I'm sure he must have the papers somewhere."

"What about his wife, could she help us?"

"Oh, no. I think that was part of the reason he moved into the upstairs on Elm Street.

When she died, I do not think he could stand to be at the house without her. In fact, you know their house still has their belongings in it. No one ever came and cleaned out either of the houses."

"Well, I'm going to try to undo all of this for the both of us. Grandmother, please, don't call Father or anyone about this right now. Do you know the addresses of the homes?"

"Why no, but I can give you directions and tell you what they look like. No one ever moved into the houses. Okay, I will let you get to work, but please do come to see me again."

"Grandmother, I will do exactly that. I love you." Robert runs down the sidewalk and waves goodbye, as he gets in his car. His grandmother smiles and watches him drive off.

Chapter 10

Saturday Morning

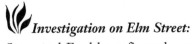

Investigation on Elm Street:

Steve and Fred have figured out the addresses of attorney's office and his residence, which had been vacant since the attorney's death. They walked a couple of blocks, through the fog that appeared out of nowhere. Fred pulls the collar of his jacket up around his neck.

"Nobody would have seen the car in this fog."

Steve nods and says, "Just need to make sure no one sees us." Steve hunches his shoulders and gives a shiver. "Jeez, this fog is weird, but perfect for sneaking into someone's abandoned house… I hope."

They wanted to be sure that the lady across the street did not see or even think that they were inside of the house.

The day before they had seen that there were steps on the back of the house going down to what seemed to be a basement. They decided it was the best way to enter, as the trees in the back of the house blocked anyone from seeing them go into the house.

Steve tested the doorknob, with his gloved hand and the door easily opened.

"It wasn't even locked! What a surprise!" They went in brushing cobwebs away and following a narrow hallway to a set of stairs that went up to the main house. As they walked to the top of the stairs, there was a narrow doorway that was a separate storage-type room. It was very narrow and filled with filing cabinets and cupboards that hung on the wall.

Steve pulls the chain on the light in the room and hands Fred a paper with names and things that would be important if they find them. Steve finds a file with Robert's grandfather's name on it and one with his grandmother's name on it. He puts them in a grocery bag that they were carrying. Steve felt people would assume they had groceries in the bag!

Fred, squints at him. "Really, no one would question us, I'm sure if you were carrying a briefcase."

Steve frowns at him. "I just don't want any problems or accusations. This is not my normal work, you know." They grab everything they think could help Robert out and did double time to get out of there before the fog lifted.

Steve and Fred decide to go have breakfast and give Robert a call.

"Robert, this is Steve. We are at this cool little restaurant just off Main Street, near Jefferson."

Robert shoots a name back to him and tells him that he and his grandfather used to go there a lot. "I'm on my way. I will get something when I get there. Steve, I do not want to go over anything there. We will do it back at the motel after we meet at the restaurant. See you in a few."

Chapter 11

Jo Jo's Bar and Grill

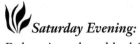*Saturday Evening:*

Robert is at the table drinking a beer and has an envelope of info his grand-mother had, which so far did not mean much of anything. He is banking that the guys will come back with better information. Steve and the other two guys walk in and join him at the table.

"Well, how did it go?" He motions for the waitress to bring a pitcher of beer.

Steve says, "Well, it was freaky, both places looked like they were still lived in, excluding the dust and cobwebs. We have newspaper clippings that may be of interest." Mike found them in the office that was used before the attorney moved into the house, which it seems he stayed in most of the time after his wife died.

This is all according to the information the neighbor lady had. She lived across the street and saw us on the porch."

"Do you think that could cause us a problem?"

"Nah, she was just a friendly old lady, and I don't think she thought anything other than we were looking for relatives."

Robert looks at him with concern. Steve puts his hand up "No, don't worry. She didn't ask us any questions. We just covered why we were there, and she was helpful." He smiled at Robert. "It's okay. No problem."

Steve hands Robert a folder with Robert's grandfathers name on it. It was a will and trust papers and some inventory of his grandfather's personal belongings.

Fred and Steve showed up with what looked like a wedding ring, not sure they should have taken that.

They also had other miscellaneous paperwork. A registration on an antique vehicle that no one actually saw.

"Okay, so Sunday, I'd like to get home by 5:00 p.m. and surprise my wife."

Fred, says, "Okay, I will drive, and you guys can just BS with each other. What time do you want to leave?"

"Let's get out of here no later than 9:00 a.m., earlier if possible. Anxious to see my wife."

Fred says, "Okay, you guys put your bags at your doorways, and I will pick up your bags by 8:00 a.m. and load them into the car; then we can eat and get an early start. We can go directly to the car after breakfast. I'm always up early."

"Well, it will take a fair amount of time. The earlier the better." They looked at each other, nodded in agreement, and got up to call it a night.

As Robert sat at the table for a moment longer, he talks out loud to himself. "Yep, this trip could give me the truth that would be a life-changing event for me and my family." Little did he know how right he might be.

He got up and smiled as he headed to his room at the motel. He picked up the phone and called Elaine to tell her he was looking forward to seeing her and that she may be surprised at what he wanted to tell her.

As he stood looking in the mirror in the motel room waiting for Elaine to answer, his face turned to a bit of a frown. "Wonder where she and girls are? Oh, well, I'll tell her tomorrow." He leaves a message on the phone telling her how anxious he is to see her.

He goes down to the bar for a drink and to take one more look at what he has found. He just gets seated at a table and sees Fred at the bar. He places the envelope he was going to look through on the chair beside him.

He waves and Fred comes over with his drink in hand and sits down. "Couldn't sleep?"

Robert smiles, "Yeah a lot to think about."

"Well, the job's done now, no worries."

Robert says one more drink and I'm done."

Fred and Robert hit it off and seem to really like each other. After a second drink, one more for Robert—one more than Robert should have had.

Robert takes his last swallow of his drink gets up and says, "I'm off, see you tomorrow. The folder is still sitting on the chair where Robert put it.

Fred nods. "I'll be following you."

Robert walks out of the bar and FFred sees envelope on the chair and quickly picks it up and puts it inside his jacket.

As soon as Robert is out of sight Fred heads to the reservation desk. The gal, he made friends with when he first got there was on duty knowing that she would be helping Fred. He hands her the envelope and tells her that he will wait. She knows she needs to copy it right away. He shows her the $50 bill that is hers if she does this right. The girl practically runs to do the copying. In a few minutes, she is back. Fred glances at the work and measures the size of each stack. Smiles, gives the girl a smile and a kiss on the cheek. Fred puts copy of papers in his bag and will put original Will into Roberts bag in the morning. He is banking that Robert will not go looking for it before then.

"Hell, with that I'll just tell him that the bartender saw it on the seat and that I picked it up for him. I'll tell him I didn't want to wake him."

The night went by quickly, Robert got up with the light flowing in through the window. He grabbed his belongings and headed out to meet the guys.

He gives Elaine a call and leaves a message that he is looking forward to seeing her this evening.

Chapter 12

Sunday Drive Home

*Early Sunday Morning:*
Fred arranges a last morning breakfast at 8:00 a.m. for the guys' last goodbyes and celebration of their journey. Each room is rung at 7:30 and told to come down to the restaurant at the motel at eight. Each will leave their door ajar and Fred will go in and get the bags that should be by the door.

The guys are up and about and put their bags out for pickup by their servant Fred. Steve says to himself, *A little strange for Fred?* Shrugs his shoulders and says, "Maybe he's changed."

Fred picks up the suitcases and replaces the folder inside of Roberts case and heads to the restaurant for breakfast. He sees, Robert.

"How are you this morning?"

Robert leans toward him and in a low voice tells him, "I misplaced all our information. I thought I had it with me at the bar and could not find it this morning. Bar is not open now. I asked the clerk she said she is a new clerk not here last night. "Robert looks defeated.

"Robert, don't worry. The bartender saw it on the chair where you left it and gave it to me. I did not want to wake you, so I just put it in your case this morning.

"You could have woken me."

"Don't think so after what you drank last night. Don't you have a headache?"

Robert grins, "Believe it or not, I don't." He smiles and Fred laughs.

"That's great!"

They head off to the restaurant for breakfast.

Breakfast was quiet, everyone trying to wake up or get over having too much to drink.

As everyone seems to be finished with their meal, Robert lets the group know that he is ready to go at any time. Everyone seems to be a bit anxious to get on the road. They all get up without a word and begin to walk out of the restaurant. On the way out, Steve hands Robert the bill. With a half a smile on this face and his head down, he keeps walking.

That Afternoon:

It is a little after noon time and the sky is cloudy and looks like it might rain. Seems like the forces were holding them back.

From the back seat, Robert says, "We will have to book it to arrive home by 5:00 p.m., almost impossible."

Fred is driving and looks in the mirror and nods. "Don't worry, we'll get there."

Robert has all the info they gathered in a large brown envelope. He thanks all the guys for their help and tells them, "you know this weekend could be the beginning of a new life for me."

The guys laugh and kid around with Robert. "Yeah, you could go home and find out the milk man took your place" or "she decides she likes being without you."

Everyone, laughs, and Robert says, "That would be the day!" He leans across the seat and tells Fred, "Is this all you've got? You drive like your grandmother!"

"Well, big shot, how soon do you want to be there, like, now I'll bet! You'll be surprised how soon you are home." Fred guns the engine and the car flies down the road.

"Now I didn't tell you to kill us! Just not to drive like your grandmother."

Fred laughs as they make the next turn. "You don't know my grandmother!"

On the very next turn the car begins to slide and heads for a guardrail, the car has lost its traction and they begin to fly over the guardrail. There is the sudden noise of the car ripping the railing. The scraping and screeching of metal tearing on the car is unbelievable.

Fred yells, "Get out, get the hell out! Jump!"

The doors fly open, and the car begins to flip end over end and down a steep embankment. The sounds echo through the canyon. The voices of the guys yelling and the shredding of the metal, as well as the motor noises. All happened within a matter of seconds and then dead silence. The air is filled with the smell of smoke and dirt. The car smashed against rocks and a tree trunk, and Fred thinks that it probably kept the car from going to the bottom of the hill. He figured that probably saved the other guys' lives. At least he hopes so.

Fred lies there trying to imagine how this will all turn out. He realizes how it is so quiet, no real noise, except for the sound of the rain that taps on the metal of the car and a slight breeze that rustles through the trees.

Fred is alive but half-in and half-out of the car. The car door is gone; however, he is pinned down by the front seat that pulled away from its floor and on top of his leg and hip. He yells, for the other guys.

Fred tells himself, "I've got to do something!"

He listens to see if he hears the other guys and with severe pain in his side and his leg, he realizes just how trapped he is in the car. He tries to move and is unable to. The creaking of the car, as he rocks and jiggles it, gives him an instant flash to stop rocking or trying to move the car, as he might cause it to roll down the hill even farther. He becomes very aware of how silent everything is and wonders how this is going to work out.

He hears no voices of distress and begins to yell to the other guys, praying for answers.

"Steve, Steve, are you out there?"

Steve yells back, "Alive can't get up yet. You, okay? I'll get us some help."

Fred doesn't reply, just begins to yell again. "Mike, Mike, you okay?" No answer, he just hears moaning coming from down the hill. "Hang in there. Steve is calling on his phone for help," he says to ease Mike's fear, hoping that he hears him. Things are quiet, just too quiet.

Steve starts yelling for Robert, over and over. No sound, he thinks, *God he can't be dead!*

Fred and Steve yell for Robert together, but there's no sound, nothing.

Steve speed dials the phone to Patrick. Patrick, picks up. "Patrick, bad news, not good."

Steve gasps for air.

Patrick says, "Steve, what's up, you okay?"

"No, not okay everyone's hurt. Can't get a response from Robert, he must be at the top somewhere. We wrecked the car and rolled down the hill about ten miles outside of town, over a guardrail."

Patrick says, "No police or anyone there, right?"

Steve whispers, "Don't think so."

"Hang in there, hold on. I'm getting you help. Are you in Robert's car?"

"Yes... think I'm passing out." Phone goes silent.

Patrick quickly puts a trace on Robert's car. He has it on all his family's cars, just so he knows everyone is okay. Robert's car comes through.

He calls his doctors and the hospital, which he owns. Another call to his private ambulance and tells them to get out there. He also contacts the emergency ambulances from the hospital that he owns. He has given the trace location of the vehicle to all, and heads immediately to the hospital that Robert will be taken to.

Janet grabs her coat and hat and runs after Patrick to the car. "Oh my God! I would have never dreamed this could happen. What about Elaine? Someone has to tell her!"

"I have called the police captain and he has already sent someone out to get Elaine."

"Patrick, you can't send your Private Ambulance out there, can you?"

"I already called it in, so the police know the ambulances are on the way. I would like to go out and see what has happened to Robert since they had no vocal contact with him."

Patrick's phone rings and it is his contact from the police department, and he is told, "We, found Robert near the top of the hill. He is alive! Your private ambulance is on the way to the hospital with just Robert. The other three guys are coming to the same hospital in the other ambulances."

Patrick sighs. "Any way you could deliver the others guy to Central Hospital and only Robert to my hospital?"

Officer replies, "Sure thing. Anything I should know?"

Patrick hesitates, then replies, "I don't want this in the news on any level. Can you manage to keep this one quiet?"

The officer replies, "Sure, no fallback on me, right?"

"I'll take care of everything; no worries as long as you do your part. If you want to feel protected bring that phone to me, get a new phone and give me the old one. Do that today and no one should even look at it."

"No, I trust you. It will be okay."

"It is imperative this does not make the news."

Patrick floors the car, wanting to get to the hospital before Robert arrives. He tells Janet, "I have a grand idea to protect us from Robert ever finding out about his grandfather."

"You, do?"

"Yes, we dug ourselves into this mess; now we have to protect ourselves."

Janet looks at him, wondering what is up next. Patrick pulls into the hospital and lets Janet out at the emergency entrance. "Go in tell them who you are and that I'm parking the car. If Elaine shows up before I join you, tell her nothing! Go with the flow of anything that goes on, follow my lead. Okay?!"

"Yes, of course."

Patrick turns out his lights as he pulls up next to the ambulance parked at the back of the hospital. Knocks twice and pushes the door open. His ambulance driver is there. "How is he? What has happened?"

"He is in with Dr. White?"

"Where?"

The driver points, and Patrick runs down the hall and into the private area where they have Robert.

"John, how is he?"

"A couple of stitches on the head, he needs rest and quiet and someone to watch over him. He has a severe concussion. Looks like he hit his head on a rock."

Patrick looks the doctor square in the eyes, "No other problems... internal or otherwise?"

"No, he is a pretty strong guy, and there is no evidence of anything other than this concussion. He will need rest and care for a while and then he should be his old self again."

"Okay, I want to take this over and have my personal doctors take care of him at my private home."

Dr. White, looks at him and says, "You must keep me advised."

"You know if anything goes wrong, you will hear from me. I pay you well enough to honor my wishes, don't I?"

The doctor nods with a half-smile. "No Recourse, I disappear from your memory, right?"

Patrick nods. "One more thing, when his wife comes in to see him this is what you need to do." He coaches the doctor. "No mess ups! Got it? An easy hundred grand for just that one conversation, not counting the rest of this service you have given me. I won't forget it!"

Patrick finds out from Dr. White that a Dr. Edwards has the other guys in his care and that they were taken to the hospital downtown that Patrick had requested. Patrick decides that he will go and see them tomorrow since all are injured but not critical. He heads back down the hall and out the door, gets in his car, and drives to the parking lot at the emergency entrance and goes inside to be with Janet.

Chapter 13

Hospital Waiting Room

Patrick enters the waiting room; he sees Janet sitting and waiting. The right nurse (who Dr. White appointed to the desk after he received Patrick's call) is at the table to greet Patrick, Janet, and Elaine when she arrives. She has a specific script so that she knows what to say and do.

Janet looks at Patrick with a question in her eyes. He smiles and says I will tell you later just go along.

They wait patiently for Elaine to arrive. Janet looks out the window of the waiting room.

"I hope Elaine is not creating a bigger problem by acting out as she does sometimes. You know demanding and not willing to listen."

Patrick shakes his head in wonderment of what Janet just said. "I don't think that will be a problem, think this may be more difficult for her than you think."

A few minutes later, Patrick gets the call from the police who were sent to pick up Elaine. They let him know that they are at Elaine's house and will pick her up unless she is not there."

Patrick tells him, "She should be there; if not, I'm really going to be upset."

"Car's here; she probably is will get back to you if a problem."

"Okay." He hangs up the phone and mumbles to himself, "She has to be there."

Chapter 14

An Unsuspected Caller

Sunday Late Afternoon:

The doorbell rings, Elaine smiles and dances to the door. "You crazy guy, you don't have to ring." Her face drops as she peers into the eyes of a police officer. "Can I help you?"

"Mrs. Robert Williams?"

"Why, yes." Her eyes widen and her breath is short. "Can I help you?"

"Mrs. Williams, I regret to tell you—"

Elaine goes weak and leans against the doorframe. Her eyes well with tears. "Yes, what is it?"

The police officer shows her his badge. "I need you to come with me to the hospital."

"Why? Everyone here is okay."

"Is your husband Robert Williams here?"

"No, no he should be here any moment... went on a business trip. He's due any moment."

She looks at the officer as he tells her that her husband will not be arriving as she thought.

She shrieks and quickly stands on her toes to look around the police officer to see if Robert is in the car. He is not! She begins to collapse, and the police officer takes her inside to sit down.

"Do you need an ambulance?"

"No, no. I'm fine. I will drive myself. She suddenly becomes very calm as if she were going to go grocery shopping. "I'll get my coat."

She closes the door, and the police officer waits outside for her. She slides down the wall and begins to sob uncontrollably and then catches herself and says, "You must take care of this. Robert needs you now!"

Elaine gets in control and grabs her coat and runs to the car. She is extremely nervous as she backs down the driveway and pulls out in front of the police car, who follows her to the hospital. Looking in the rearview mirror, she questions herself as to why they do not go around her. She quickly makes a mental agreement with herself that they are just doing their job and that she will not fret. The police car follows her into the emergency parking lot. Elaine pulls into the lot and almost forgets to turn off the engine.

She tells herself, "You must get a hold of yourself!" She runs through the emergency door and first thing she sees is Patrick! Panting and almost out of breath as she tries to contain herself, she asks, "Patrick, what happened? Where is Robert?"

Patrick steps back and says, "He's in with the doctor. We are waiting to hear something."

Elaine shakes her head, looking at Patrick. "This can't be true! Maybe it is a mistake?"

Janet goes over to Elaine, hugging her and seems incredibly sad. Janet and Patrick, surround Elaine with their hugs!

Patrick pats her back and whispers, "He doesn't look too good."

"Patrick, how did you guys get here so quickly? Did someone call you?"

"I was called."

"You haven't seen him?"

Patrick looks down at the floor. "Only when they wheeled him in. He seemed to be unconscious."

"Patrick, who called you? Who knew?"

"One of the neighbors phoned me and told me where he saw the car." Patrick was saying that to protect himself from questions from Elaine. As an afterthought he also told her that Steve had called from the accident site. He explained it was then that he went into full action to get them help as fast as possible. We came here immediately after that. I called the police to go and get you."

Elaine goes over to the nurses' desk. "I'm Mrs. Williams, Robert Williams's wife. I need to see him, or the doctor now."

The nurse tells her she will check. She makes a call and tells Elaine he is with the doctor. As Elaine walks away from the desk, she tells the nurse, "I need to know what happened right away."

Patrick walks over and puts his arm around her. He steers her back to the chairs in the waiting room.

A few minutes later, the nurse walks over to them and tells them that she is sorry and has no information for them and that Dr. White will be with them shortly.

Elaine tells her, "Someone, better be! I have a right to know how he is, after all I am his wife." Elaine looks around the waiting room and finds it strange that they are the only ones there. It is too much for her to think about or even ask about. She is exhausted with fear of what might have happened to Robert.

As each minute drags by, Elaine becomes more and more agitated. "I've had it!" She jumps up and pushes through the swinging door. Dr. White has been advised and is running up the hall to meet her.

"Mrs. Williams?"

"Yes."

The doctor keeps walking down the hallway so she will follow. "You know your husband was in a terrible automobile accident?"

"Yes, what is wrong with him? What happened?"

"Mrs. Williams, I'm sorry but your husband was severely injured, and we could not save him. I am deeply sorry."

Elaine screams with tears rolling down her face. "I want to see my husband!"

"Mrs. Williams, we cannot do that. Your husband was killed in the accident. His head was crushed, and he probably died instantly." She struggles to get away from the doctor to search for her husband. The doctor waves to a nurse coming up the hall who gives Elaine a shot in the arm, which immediately puts her into a relaxed state. The doctor leads her to some chairs in the hall.

Elaine now, calm, asks, "When can arrangements be made to bring him from the hospital."

"No need to worry. His father has already taken care of that."

"What? Did he see Robert?"

"He was here when the ambulance brought him in. Please take care and know that all the best is going to happen for your husband. We regret that you have had to go through this." The doctor walks her back to the Emergency Room where Patrick and Janet meet her.

Janet says, "Don't worry. We will take care of everything."

Elaine weeps, "He is my husband. I should be doing that."

Janet puts her arm around Elaine's waist and walks with her to the door. "Honey, everything will be okay."

Elaine once again musters up her strength and pulls away from them and announces she is going home to take care of the family she has left.

She runs across the parking lot and cries in the car for several minutes and then gets her act together and drives to her house. The children are at the neighbors'; she does not want to tell her story to them. She calls her mom and in tears says, "Mom, Mom, Robert had an accident. He's dead!"

Her mother gasps, "Oh, my God!"

Elaine sobs uncontrollably and asks her mom to come and get the children from the next-door neighbors, and to take them to her house. "Please do not tell them that anything is wrong. I will call you in the morning, Mom." Her mother agrees.

On the way home from the hospital, Elaine reviews in her mind all that has happened over the past day or two. Everything has happened so very quickly and unexpectedly. Wiping the tears from her eyes, she reminds herself to take things one moment at a time so she can really figure out what needs to be done for her to be able to find out the truth. about Robert.

She is convinced that something has happened to Robert, but she does not believe that he is dead. Speaking out loud to herself she says, "There is a voice in me and a strong feeling that Robert is alive somewhere!"

As she reviews in her mind the past few days, she realizes that she was shut out and had no personal contact with anyone. Not the minister, police, or hospital. All was handled without Elaine even knowing what was going on. She spent the first two days, in her room crying and sleeping with tranquilizers that the doctor had given her. Her plan was to, on the third day, go and make the arrangements and talk to the mortuary and funeral parlor.

However, on the second day she was told the funeral would be the following day and that she was to attend. She was appalled and asked Janet, "Why would you think I would not attend my husband's funeral! I hate the fact that you thought you would take all of this over and never consult me!"

Janet, as apologetic as she could be, said, "Why, honey, we just wanted to make things easier for you." Elaine nods and walks away.

She was hurt and angry that everything was taken out of her hands. She was determined to find out why she so quickly and easily was not allowed to tend to her own husband's funeral. Luckily, they did not know about Robert's life Insurance policy that was with an attorney he met through his job. The thought of doing anything about his life insurance never entered her mind. She wondered if Patrick even knew.

She doubted that Patrick would know, since she never saw Robert's policy or had any idea of what he wanted. This is something she felt in time she would investigate. Hopefully, without Patrick knowing or being involved.

Chapter 15

Home Alone

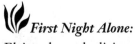***First Night Alone:***

Elaine closes the living room curtain and puts the lamp on low. She just does not want the house to feel empty. She already feels lost and empty and unsure of herself.

She pours herself a glass of red wine thinking that it might help her fall asleep and that perhaps in the morning she will find out that all of this is just an awfully bad dream.

As she heads upstairs, she debates if she wants to sleep in the bed or not. As she looks in the mirror, she wipes away her tears and tells herself to just go to sleep and all will be better in the morning.

This is the last thing Elaine remembers before the day of her husband's funeral This is an unexplained nightmare for her. She never saw her husband again after the morning he left on his adventure.

Chapter 16

Return to Reality

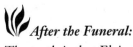 *After the Funeral:*

The truth is that Elaine has fallen asleep in her car after the funeral and was reliving the past few days. She jumps and awakens in her car when the sound of squealing tires from someone on the street driving by. She awakens and screams out, "No!" She then realizes that she had fallen asleep, listening to the water flowing in the creek. A reminder comes across her and she weeps at the acknowledgment that Robert was in an accident that supposedly took his life. As she starts to get lost in her grief, she remembers that she was supposed to be at a reception for Robert's death.

She sits up straight in her car and says, "My God, I'm sure I'm late to the reception. Janet will be so angry."

She quickly puts the car in gear telling herself that she must at least make an appearance, or she will never hear the end of it from Janet. As Elaine arrives at Patrick and Janet's house, she turns the engine off and coasts up to the curb, as if no one will notice that she has not been there.

Elaine quietly opens the front door and sneaks in and quietly walks close to the wall heading toward the kitchen, hoping she will not be noticed.

The living and dining room is filled with people. All the right people, milling about and giving condolences. Janet just eats up all the attention and Patrick is acting much like a hand-shaking politician. It almost seems like they are holding a reception for their son's graduation from college rather than one for his death.

As Elaine moves along the wall, two older ladies whom she does not know, pay their condolences to her. She nods and heads for the kitchen and sees her mother sitting just outside the doorway on a stool. She grabs her mom's hand and says, "Why Barbara, how nice to see you."

She pushes open the kitchen door and pulls her mom in with her.

Barbara says, "Fine and you?"

Elaine smiles. "Mom, I'm incredibly happy to see you and need your help. It looks like a party out there instead of a funeral reception, and I don't know any of those people. I'll bet Robert doesn't either."

Her mom looks at her, smiling and wanting to crack a joke, but thinks maybe the timing would be wrong, so she lets her daughter go on.

"Look, Mom I need you to help me with the girls. I don't think they really know what has happened and that their father is not coming home. I would like you to get the girls out of here and take them to your house to spend the night. I will call you in the morning and come over."

Barbara agrees and heads out to get the girls. She will let Patrick and Janet know that she is taking the girls to her house per Elaine's request.

Elaine has a plan to get to her mom's in the morning and then take the girls to school. Afterwards, she wants to go to the police department for records of the accident and names of officers who were there.

Her plan was to find out what happened to her husband's car? Who the guys were that were in the car with Robert and where they are now? She wants to visit the mortuary and find out who took care of Robert and who made the arrangements for Robert's burial? Since she never got to see Robert, she wants to know was he buried or cremated? All this information has never been given to her. Let alone a long conversation with Robert's parents about all that they did. When she had tried to talk to them, both would busy themselves with something else and always tell her not to worry.

She wants to find out who got Robert's car off the crash site and where it was taken. She is hoping that if she could see the car that she may be able to find papers in the car that would let her know what they had been doing. She will go through her husband's home office and perhaps talk with his attorney to see if anything can be brought to light. Exhausted from all her thinking, she is happy to get home. It seemed to take her a short time to return home; it must have been caused by all the thinking she had been doing.

She arrives home and heads upstairs to shower and go to bed as she is very, very tired. Almost too tired to feel broken and sad.

She whispers to herself, "Must sleep and not think any more tonight. Maybe, this is all a bad, bad, dream."

Elaine lays in her bed with pillows all around her; she looks out the window and sees a gentle glow from the moon shining in her room. She begins to dose off and suddenly feels as though someone is in the room! With a start, she props herself up on the pillows, eyes wide open with a startled look. There was a haze or maybe it was a glow from the moonlight.

Elaine stares steadily and says, "Robert, is that you?" The mist clears. "Robert, where are you?" Robert seems to fade into the mist and yet, seems to be beckoning her to come to him. She hears his voice, far off.

"Find me."

Elaine says, "I don't know how, but I won't give up and I will find you if you are still here with us." Elaine wonders if she is asleep and dreaming, and not fully awake. She closes her eyes and falls into a deep sleep.

Chapter 17

The Morning After the Funeral

As the morning sun begins to rise, the light through the window awakens Elaine, and she stretches and listens to hear if her family is up already. She wonders if Robert has fed the kids. She gets out of bed and goes to the bathroom to see if Robert is in the shower.

"No, no one there." She grabs her robe and goes downstairs to see what the girls are doing and finds, with shock, no one is there.

She begins to panic and then the phone rings. She runs to answer it, thinking that Robert must have the girls with him. "Hello, Robert, where are you?"

"Elaine, this is Mom. What are you talking about?"

"Oh, Mom I thought it was Robert?"

Her mother begins to worry and talk very slowly. "Elaine, I have the girls. Do you remember, you were coming over today so we could find out what happened to Robert?" The phone goes silent.

"Robert... he's at work."

Barbara now really concerned. "Elaine, could you come over to my house now? There is something I'd like to show you and talk to you about."

"Sure, Mom I will be there very soon."

"Good! Now quickly, dress and come over. I want to show you something."

"On my way." The phone hangs up.

Barbara is extremely worried. It seems that Elaine has blocked out the funeral and what has happened. Barbara sips her coffee wondering what she should do. She decides if Elaine arrives still thinking nothing has happened that she will have to take her to the cemetery and see if that solves the problem.

Elaine comes in the front door, looking very forlorn and sad. "Mom." She hugs her mom and begins to cry and cry. Barbara just holds her until she gets it all out.

Barbara asks her if she wants coffee, she declines and quickly wipes her eyes as she sees the two girls coming down the stairs. Both run over and hug her.

"We love you very much. Don't cry we both know that Daddy will come back to us."

Elaine hugs and kisses and kisses the girls. "You are the best, my gifts from God, my angels."

Mandy, gives her mom a smile and a wink and says, "Angels never lie, they make dreams come true that bring us happiness."

Barbara silently thanks God.

Elaine says, "I know I, just for a bit, was not sure about anything. My mind had me forget the past two days and believe that nothing happened. Then it hit me one more time and everything came flooding in." She glances at her daughters. "Do you girls want to go to school today and Grandma and I will pick you up this afternoon. Maybe, we can all go for a milkshake after school. Are you in?" Both girls smile and nod. "Run get dressed and we will go." Elaine turns back to her mother. "Mom after we get the girls to school, we will go to the library and make a list of things we need to do."

"Why the library?"

"For some research."

Chapter 18

Looking for the Truth

"We are going to become partners in finding out what really happened to Robert."

Barbara is pretty much going along with all this research because she is not sure that Elaine is ready to accept anything more and hopes that the clues will bring her into realization. For now, she wants to be her ally and her best friend.

"I want to go to the newspaper and find out what story they wrote, as I have not seen anything in the news about an accident on that road."

Barbara nods and says, "We can do all of this, but I don't think it will bring Robert back."

Elaine nods. "That's right because I don't believe he is dead. Not when I just spoke to Robert last night."

Barbara looks over the top of her glasses in shock. "What are you talking about?"

Elaine scoots up next to her mom at the kitchen table. "You are not going to believe this!" Elaine proceeds to tell Barbara about the meeting with Robert in the haze of her bedroom and what he said. Barbara is flabbergasted and looks at her daughter and decides it is best to let her know that she will support her on whatever she wants to do.

At this point Barbara is thinking maybe best to play it out with her than to make her think otherwise.

"Mom, I want us to sit down together and think about what all the missing pieces are. Maybe we can figure out why we did not get to see the body. I want to know why none of Robert's belonging were given to me except for the wallet that the officer brought to the door. I am not even sure if that was the wallet that was Robert's. It was a light-colored brown and not the dark wallet that he was using that I had given him. There are a lot of pieces missing in this puzzle."

Barbara now is beginning to think that Elaine is on to something. "Okay, so let us make a plan."

Elaine jumps up and says, "I think you and I should go back out to where the accident happened and search for anything we can find. I know on that hillside and gully that no one probably went out to clear the area, other than dragging the car out of there."

Barbara scoots closer to Elaine and nods. "I'm ready when you are. When did you want to do this?"

"I'd like to do it tomorrow while the girls are in school. We'll take them to the bus stop and then be on our way, okay?"

"Okay, I'll be ready with some bags to put anything in that we may find, and then we can come back here and go over everything. They smile at each other, exchanging a hug and handshake.

Chapter 19

Crash Site

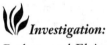*Investigation:*

Barbara and Elaine pull up to the crash site and park Barbara's Pathfinder off to the side of the road. They each have small bags to put things in they might find.

"Mom, you take the upper half, pick up anything you can find that looks like it could have something to do with the accident or something that any of the guys may have had in their pockets. I'm going all the way down as far as I can and still be able to climb back up. By the way, Mom, did you ever hear anything about the guys who were with Robert?"

"Matter of fact, I did not!"

"Hmm...."

"For God's sake be careful!"

The bent and twisted guardrail still has not been repaired. Elaine carefully climbed over and moved down and across the hill.

Barbara looks near the top. She finds a broken watch and some gold coins that she stuffs into her pockets. Elaine has found torn papers and is stuffing her pockets with them.

The sound of a car pulling up to the guardrail gets Barbara's attention. She looks up and, to her surprise, Patrick steps out of the car and is walking over to the guardrail and looking down the hill. Elaine hears the echo of the car door slamming and shields her eyes from the sunlight as she looks up the hill to see who is getting out of the car. Elaine realizes it is Patrick and thinks, *Not Patrick, anyone but Patrick!*

Patrick, yells down the hill, "Is that you, Elaine?"

Elaine yells back, "Is that you, Patrick? What are you doing here?"

"I might ask you the same thing."

Barbara see's what is going on and finds her way back to the road and drives their car slowly toward the guardrail.

Elaine yells up to Patrick, as she starts to climb back up the hill, "I had to see for myself that this really happened! It's hard to believe, you know?"

Patrick waves her to come on up. "This can't be good for you."

Barbara yells down the hill trying to make a cover for Elaine. "I thought you were just going to look over the rail, not go down the hill. Patrick, why are you here?"

"Ladies, I saw your car, and thought maybe someone had a problem. Then I looked down and there was Elaine, being where she shouldn't be."

Elaine climbs back over the railing brushing her clothes off.

"We'd better go. We have got to pick up the girls from school." She begins to walk away from Patrick and then turns back and asks him, "What are you doing out here?"

He smiles, and says, "I have an appointment I have to get to." Patrick looks at Elaine with a frown. "You have got to move forward. There is nothing to prove. It was an accident; that is all." Patrick jumps in his vehicle and goes one direction, as Barbara and Elaine go in the opposite direction.

Elaine looks over at Barbara as they start down the road. "Wonder what he was doing out here? Wonder if he was really coming to the site for some reason?"

Barbara shakes her head. "Probably doing what he said. He was going to an appointment... until he saw us." The rest of the drive was considerably quiet.

It was evident that they both did not think the same way about this subject. Barbara was bit less suspicious than her daughter.

Chapter 20

Private Meeting

 Small Café:

Patrick drives an hour from where the crash happened. He is to meet up with Fred who has now recovered from his injuries at the accident. Patrick walks in and sees Fred drinking coffee on the other side of the room. Fred looks up and smiles. Patrick stretches out his hand and says, "How you are doing?"

"Okay, whole plan didn't come off exactly as I thought. I think driving on the racetrack is a better bet for me. Did Robert get transported okay?"

Patrick takes a seat across from Fred. "First of all, I want you to know, I don't think this accident was your fault, just too rainy. You driving too fast is your fault, but I'm not blaming you. Robert would have been fine except for the severe concussion he has."

Fred, looking for assurance. "He's okay?"

"Yes, he's fine, a bit of amnesia, and a while to recover."

Fred leans forward and quietly says, "Well, the plan you had for recovery of information from Robert was a bust and me driving didn't solve anything either. I heard Mike is okay and going home soon, maybe even tomorrow. Steve is pretty laid up I heard."

Patrick tells him, "Steve is on the mend and will be okay." Patrick stands up. "Why do you think I had to do this, you fool! You were the one who no one really knew, and I needed you for that reason so the information you gathered would mean nothing to you and go nowhere else. Not sure if I'll ever know what was in those papers or find anything out. I don't like the fact that I hired you to sabotage my son finding out the truth, but I'm not going to lose everything I have for anyone!"

Fred gets up shakes his head and begins to walk away, "No problem here. I know nothing. Never even glanced at the documents." Fred just keeps walking toward the door.

Patrick yells after him, "Be gone tomorrow!"

Fred nods and says, "No problem."

Patrick walks over to Fred and says in a low voice, "No problem, unless you don't keep your mouth shut! Don't want to hear or see that you are back in this area again."

"You've got it, no worries?"

Patrick says, "Send me an address and I'll send you a bonus."

Fred just keeps walking, knowing that Patrick's bonus may not be what one would typically think. He is being paid to know nothing about anything and he is happy to do that, knowing that the bonus will really be a payoff for being quiet and disappearing.

Fred knew he would never cross Patrick and did not want any part of that. He liked life too much to deal with Patrick's wrath. Being out of the area was no big deal for him. Patrick is good for his word once he gives it. It is not easy to find the generosity in someone such as Patrick, but he is good for his word, good or bad. You just don't question it.

Chapter 21

Morning Meeting

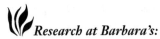*Research at Barbara's:*

Elaine and Barbara have emptied the envelope out on the table and spread out everything they found. Within the bits and pieces of paper that had been torn it looked like there may have been a part of a will or something that had the word *Estate* on it and part of a page with Robert's name on it. No full sentences or full documents.

There was a brown wallet that Elaine was sure was not Robert's. The best thing with the most proof was the broken pocket watch that Barbara found. That was for sure Robert's.

Problem with the watch it was only the cover of the watch not the whole thing.

"No one can say Robert wasn't in the car. However, one could just discard it, because there was only just a piece of the cover of the watch."

"Mom, we can't give up. Maybe we should go out there again."

Barbara says, "I think we need to find out what happened to the car. What tow places might have it."

Elaine hands her mom a list of places. "I've called these and either get no answer or someone saying they don't have it. Maybe we could make friends with one of those guys and have them see if they can find it. I know the license plate number and what the car looks like. I'll bet I even have a picture of it. I'm going out to the junkyards and see if I can find it."

Barbara says, "Something to think about; it sounds good, but even if we find it that just confirms he was in the accident. I thought you wanted to prove he was still alive?"

"I do, but I need to know what really happened and why someone would want to make him disappear from his life completely!"

"Well, the hospitals seem to be no help. I cannot even get a copy of his records. Everything was supposedly given to Patrick. He said he would make a copy for me, but never did. Says I should just let go of all of this. I just can't do that."

"I think we found one of the most important things, and that is that Robert keeps contacting us. Mandy told me the other day she was looking at a magazine and the page, by itself, seemed to flip over and there was a beach with white sand and blue ocean and that her dad told her "this is where I am. Have Mommy find me."

"My God is he being held somewhere and needs help? I just can't give up yet. I know it now. It has been almost a year that we have been searching and asking questions with no good answers. I do know that part of the burned papers could have been a will, according to what wills look like, however, there is no information that we could follow."

Barbara says, "I think the only ones who will know are probably Janet and Patrick, as they seem to be the only direct link, and you know they are not going to tell us anything."

Elaine agrees. "But the reality is they are not talking! The only reason they would be doing this is so there would be no inheritance to Robert. I do believe that envelope had the Will that gave that inheritance to Robert. For all I know they somehow took it and blew it! I know that it sounds so negative regarding them, but I have to say they never mentioned anything about a Will, or anything being left to Robert, their favorite grandchild! I've been amazed that we have been able to hang on to the house."

"Robert didn't make a lot of money, but he did take care of us with his annuities and insurance. He did pay our house this past year, so that is security. I don't like living here without him. It's just too difficult."

Barbara hesitated to say what she was thinking, but felt she must. "Elaine, I just think there has to come a time that things must come to an end."

"I know you do, and I'm thinking about it, something just keeps telling me to not give up and to not let it consume me, which it already has. I would like to sue the police force, hospital, and all for not letting me, his wife, handle his funeral, and everything else. Patrick just took over and that was that. No questions, with regard to what I wanted for my husband. There was no one willing to speak to me about any part of his medical care in the hospital, or anything after that. I can't help but wonder why we can't even find the remains of the car. It's all so ridiculous."

Barbara gives her thoughts, hoping to help Elaine sort things out. "Well, you know he is a wealthy man and has a lot of businesses and pull in this town. I really believe his money talks. You know he is given whatever cooperation he wants. Probably from most bureaucrats in this town and probably a few other places as well."

"My question is what would he have done with Robert? He surely must be well by now. I cannot imagine him wanting to just forget about us. Mom, maybe we should have the grave opened up and see if he is in the casket."

"Elaine did you forget that Patrick had him cremated and put in the casket?"

"Oh my God, I feel so helpless. How could this happen?"

Barbara takes Elaine's hand and says, "Why don't we take a break and just let things settle down a bit for about six months and then see where things are? I'm not telling you to give up but to clear your head, relax, and see what the next six months brings."

Elaine picks up everything they have been looking at and puts it in a box and up on the shelf in her living room closet.

"We have had all the investigation ventures with no real satisfaction. Okay, I'll give it six months to only casually looking at it and wondering about what we found. I know if I'm not careful it will consume my life and not be good for me or the girls."

Elaine hugs her mom and gets the girls and heads for the door. She tells the girls to get in the car and quickly goes over to the closet and grabs the box she put on the shelf. Her mom looks at her over the top of her glasses.

Elaine smiles. "Just in case I might get an idea and want to look at something."

Barbara nods and says, "Remember our agreement six months. Put them where you will and forget about it."

Elaine smiles and skips like a teenage girl out to the car. As Barbara watches them drive away, she tells herself "At least they are all smiling. Think I'll say a little prayer to Robert tonight."

Chapter 22

Home Sweet Home

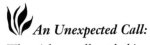*An Unexpected Call:*

The girls are all settled in their beds, and the house feels very serene and comfortable. Elaine settles into the sofa and puts her feet up on the coffee table. The phone rings, and when Elaine answers, she hears Patrick's voice on the other end.

"Patrick, is that you?"

He is breathless and with a shaky voice, he says, "Elaine, Elaine. Janet, Janet she's in the hospital. She had a stroke." Patrick begins to cry.

"Patrick, I'm so sorry. Are you at the hospital? Do you want me to come?"

"No, no there's nothing you can do."

Elaine feels deeply sorry and sad for Patrick. She never thought that would be her reaction.

"Patrick, you could come and stay at the house with me and not be alone."

"No, no I want to be in our home, but I'm going to stay at the hospital tonight. Elaine, it does not look good." He begins to sob. "If I lose her, I don't know what I'll do. She has been my whole life."

Elaine is trying not to weep for Patrick and once again tells him how sorry she is and that if he needs anything to just call. "Patrick, I do understand your grief."

As Patrick hangs up the phone, he says, "Now, I understand yours."

Patrick returns to Janet's hospital room and sits down patting her hand.

Janet whispers to him, "Maybe this is what we get for wanting it all. It all seems so unnecessary now."

Patrick, a little confused, asks her "What are you talking about?"

Janet says, "Patrick, we should have done what was right. Robert deserves what was rightfully his. I know I pushed you too hard and wanted too much. I know it now."

"Janet, it is done now; there is no undoing it."

Janet squeezes Patrick hand. "Give Robert what is his. We have enough put away to live comfortably. Just give Elaine the envelope. Let them figure it out. Let them do what they will."

Patrick nods, extremely sad and willing to do anything for her. He looks at her and says, "I never really realized how very much I loved you until now. I really love and need you to be with me."

Chapter 23

A Rude Awakening

 *Hospital Visit:*

Janet has been in the hospital for three months now, and they are not sure if she will be coming home. Elaine has just parked her car and is heading for the hospital doors when she sees Patrick walking toward her. She waves and says, "Hello, how are you? It's good to see you."

Patrick takes her hand and holds it as he smiles at her.

"Good to see you too. I've been wanting to talk to you."

Elaine steps back, as this is a bit strange for Patrick. He is normally stand-offish.

"Patrick, I thought I'd stop by and say goodbye to the two of you."

"We are leaving for the Caribbean."

Patrick smiles and says, "I hate to see you and the children go. I'll miss you."

Elaine is surprised that Patrick would say something like that. It is just not his style. She proceeds to tell him how she no longer feels there is anything here for her, since Robert seems to not be coming back. She never for a moment had believed that he was dead.

"I just can't accept Patrick that your son is dead. I just feel like he is alive somewhere, someplace." Tears well up in her eyes as she tries to hide her emotions.

She points to the hospital and says, "I should tell Janet goodbye."

Patrick tells her that Janet is asleep now. His voice is low and very depressed and hopeless.

"What do the doctors say, Patrick?"

"They say it is up to her, they really can't say if she will make it or not. At times I think she is there and wants to live and other times, I just do not know. She is very detached."

Patrick perks up a bit putting his arm around her and starts walking with her. "Let me take you to Café Serenity on the lake; you might say our last supper together. I'll let you give me a ride in your sports car." Elaine nods in agreement and then both smile.

"It's peaceful there and we can talk."

Elaine thinks to herself, *Patrick having lunch and sitting and talking with me? A real first! Of course, Patrick is not himself. He seems quite broken. Very Strange.*

They arrive at the restaurant, and the people greet them with a smile and tell Patrick that his private table is available. It is a beautiful table near the window overlooking a lake.

They take their seats, and Patrick reaches out and pats Elaine's hand and then quickly pulls it back.

The waitress arrives and they order. Elaine thinks how interesting, he is only having a salad. She follows suit. She is watching the sad face of Patrick and guessing he is just too depressed. "Patrick, I'm really sorry to hear about Janet." He nods and forces almost a smile but doesn't quite make it.

"Elaine, Janet may not make it through the night. She wanted me to do something for her after she had her stroke, something that I did not do right away. I now know that it must be done. Elaine, you had asked me if I could help you with your doubts about Robert's death. I can."

Elaine looks at him with a frown on her face. "What do you mean?"

Chapter 24

A Doorway Opened

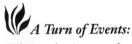 *A Turn of Events:*

"Elaine, don't go to the Caribbean, go to St. Thomas. A man named Jama will meet you and lead you to all the information you want to know.

Elaine's voice begins shaking on the verge of crying, tears begin running down her face. "What are you talking about? Are you talking about Robert? Do you know where he is?"

"Elaine, Janet and I have made a lot of mistakes and probably the biggest one most recently."

"Patrick, what have you done? Where is my husband? Do you know?"

Patrick hands her an envelope and a key, tells her to open the letter after she leaves and to just follow what Jama tells her.

"He will take you to our private island off the coast of St. Thomas."

"Your private Island? Robert never said you had an Island."

"Elaine there is a lot that Robert never knew about. Just do as I say, and you will understand everything. I'm going back to the hospital to be with Janet. I need to be with her for the time we have left. I am deeply sorry."

Patrick immediately walks out of the restaurant and a car is waiting for him to take him back to the hospital. He gives a wave as they drive off.

Elaine runs out to her car, phones her mom. Almost screaming into the phone along with crying. "Mom, I've got it! I've got the answer. Start packing. I'll be there very soon!"

She begins to laugh. "Mom, we are on our way to the truth about Robert!"

She hangs up and floors it out of the parking lot. The trip home seems to just fly by.

Chapter 25

St. Thomas

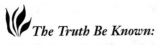 **The Truth Be Known:**

The flight to St. Thomas was smooth and no problems. When they reached the motel, the room was already paid for. The next morning Elaine is supposed to meet this man called Jama. Barbara and the children are having breakfast on the patio. Elaine motions for her mom to come inside so they could talk.

"Well, today is the day I find out what I need to know about Robert. I am nervous and a little afraid of what I might hear. I will walk down to the dock and wait for this Jama person. He is supposed to show me everything I need to know."

Barbara reminds her to call her regularly so she will not worry and will know what is going on.

"You know, Mom, I think for maybe the first time in Patrick's life he may just be doing something right and good."

Elaine kisses the girls and reminds them to behave and that she will be back very soon. She also says, "I may have some very good information about Daddy!" The girls smile. Mandy hugs her and says, "Mom, I know you will. Kiss Daddy for me."

Elaine leaves and walks down to the dock overlooking a beautiful blue cove.

An Asian man gets off a beautiful sailboat and is walking toward her. Jama greets Elaine with a bow and has her walk with him while he is carrying her belongings to the boat. Elaine is a bit nervous. She asks, "Who are you?"

"Mr. Patrick's houseboy. I take you to his house."

Elaine asks, "Why am I going there?"

Jama tells her he has a box for the key that she has that will show her important papers.

"What papers, Jama. Do you know, Robert?"

"Missy, you wait and see. Mr. Robert came here as a little boy."

The rest of the trip across the beautiful blue water is very quiet with no conversation, only the gentle sound of the boat moving across the water. Elaine's mind is going nonstop trying to figure out what is coming. What if Robert is waiting on shore for her? What will she say or do? In the distance, she sees a white plantation-style home, kind of sitting on its own piece of land on the water. She thinks, *Well, that could be considered an island.* Sure enough a few minutes later the boat begins to dock at this house. "Yep, it's an island."

Elaine follows Jama ashore, and he takes her into the house through a kitchen and into a hallway and opens a door. He motions for her to go in. She jumps back from the doorway and shakes her head no. She is not sure if she is being trapped by Patrick to get her out of the way or just being hospitable.

Jama asks if she wants to rest. She says, "No, take me to the kitchen." Jama gives her a strange look and shows her the table, and he gets her a glass of iced tea. He takes the key from her and leaves the room.

While Jama is gone with the key, she gets up and peeks around the house without going down the dark hallway where that bedroom was. It truly seems like a lovely home with lots of windows and beautiful views of the ocean, sky, and landscape.

As she sits back down in the kitchen, Jama appears with a wooden box and he opens the box with the key and tells her to see what is in it. He bows and walks backward away from her and out of the room.

Elaine opens the box and peers in. A shocked expression crosses her face, eyes wide, as she flips through a box of papers with a lot to look at. She puts on the table her findings. She is shocked to see a will, stocks, bank books, deeds, and many other documents.

She opens one bank book with a balance in the millions! She stares at a letter from Patrick.

She yells for Jama, and he quickly, appears. "Yes, Missy?"

"You, must explain, what is all of this?"

Jama tells her, "You read, and Mister Patrick's counselor will be here soon."

Elaine nods and Jama leaves the room. Elaine reads the letter and takes her phone out on the veranda to phone her mom.

"Come on, Mom, you have to be there, I need you." One more ring and her mom answers. "Mom, I know Robert is here, somewhere. I have seen the will of Robert's grandfather that leaves everything to Robert! Nothing to Patrick!" Barbara gasps at the other end of the phone.

"Oh my gosh, why now?"

"Mom, it's clear now. Patrick is losing the thing he cared about most, Janet. She had not died before I left, but he certainly acted like she was on her last leg and would die very soon. He was the most remorseful that I ever would have believed he could be. Their plan, I'm pretty sure, was to make Robert forget his life and give him a new life without us! A life they could control and have no worries about the estate."

Barbara tells her she wants to hear about everything when she gets back and would rather not talk about all of this on the phone. Elaine tells her not to tell the girls anything until she lets her know it is okay.

"I've got to hang up. Patrick's counselor is here. Bye."

Elaine looks through the window from the veranda and notices the shadow of a man standing at the front door screen, looking into the house. Elaine goes over and opens the door.

He greets her, saying hello and tells her that Patrick asked him to meet with her and go over all the documents.

"You are Elaine?" She nods yes. They go into the library and each sit on one side of the desk and he takes the box and begins to go through the documents.

After he is done explaining all the things in the box. He gets up to leave, and Elaine says,

"Wait a minute. From what I understand, Patrick stole everything that was rightfully Robert's from him and drugged him to keep him from ever finding out the truth about his inheritance. Does he really expect not to pay for this?"

Counselor Bates stands up and says, "I'm only here to explain what is in the box. It is worth almost a billion dollars or more when you look at everything in that box. Patrick is also giving this entire island to Robert. I would say that is quite an apology from a man who really does not show much emotion. You, my good woman, and your family are extremely wealthy."

Elaine gets up and says, "I suppose that all of this is to pay for the love and life that he took away from Robert. Now he has eliminated this man's wife, children, and memories that were truly his. Quite a pay off!"

Counselor Bates walks out of the room and toward the door and says, "I'm only the messenger."

She follows him into the living room and without ever looking back he walks out the front door and heads for the dock.

Chapter 26

A Love Lost

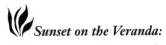*Sunset on the Veranda:*

Elaine is out on the veranda sitting, pacing, looking at her watch. Being her old impatient self, the person she has become since she lost her husband.

Wondering what she should expect. Will it really be Robert? Or will it be someone here just to let her down easily?

She is on the veranda watching the sunset when Jama comes in with a plate of fresh fruit and iced tea with lemon. He smiles and tells her the small plate of lemon cookies are his favorite. He quickly exits the room.

A couple of minutes later a tall, tan beautiful-looking man walks out onto the veranda dressed in white shirt and pants. He has long hair and looks totally like an island person. His eyes are as blue as Robert's were; with the tan, his eyes even look bluer.

Robert gives her a hug and smells her hair holding on to her a little longer than normal. He steps back and asks, "Do I know you? When I hug you and smell your hair, it seems familiar. I don't know why."

She steps back from Robert and looks at him long and hard. She is trying to make sure it is Robert, as his appearance has changed so much. It is a wise wonderful change, much more carefree.

"Robert, we do know each other and have been friends for a very long time."

Robert pulls a chair up beside her and looks at her closely. A bit of a frown, and he says, "Something seems familiar but not sure what it is."

Robert explains to her that he had been in an accident a while ago and does not remember some things. "I think I will be better soon."

"Does it make you sad not to be able to remember?"

"No, you see I don't miss what I don't know. Even though at times, I feel that there is something missing that I should know."

"Are you happy?"

"Yes, I've always been pretty happy. I have lived here most of my life. Maybe tomorrow we could go out on the boat to the island and I'll show you what I do."

Elaine smiles, "Yes, that would be interesting."

"Well, nice meeting you. I am going for a walk along the beach. Would like to go with me? It is really beautiful at sunset."

She stands up and takes his hand with a smile on her face.

The walk was nice and just chitchat, nothing serious. She wanted him to get more comfortable with her before she told him too much.

The evening ends with both parting and going their separate ways. Elaine in her room begins to put together all the information that she wants to give to Robert. She really believes it will change everything for the better.

She cannot fall asleep fast enough wanting the next morning of investigation to get underway.

As soon as morning comes, Elaine heads to the kitchen and is just about ready to have a cup of coffee when Robert walks in.

He gives her a big smile and a cheerful hello. "Are you ready?"

"Well, I was just going to…. Yes, let's go." Suddenly the coffee was not important.

They just walked along the beach picking up stones and shells and throwing them back into the water. There was a breeze and most of the way, Robert held her hand. She loved that.

Robert has been longing for a friend and someone to do things with. It seems like since he has been at the island, the only thing he has done is work.

Robert tells her, "Let's go back and change. I want to take you to the island before noon. I like to show you some of my businesses before everyone takes a work break."

"A work break, what is that?"

He throws a rock up in the air and gives a big smile "It's like, you know, a siesta. Nap time. Crazy, but great!"

They run back to the house and get ready to go. He gets dressed in dark slacks and white shirt. Casual but looks more businesslike than yesterday. Elaine has on a white flowing dress and has pulled her hair up on her head.

Elaine is quite aware of how he is smiling all the time and seems so happy. She does not remember him being this happy before.

She shudders at the thought that maybe he is better off here than at home where they used to live. Perhaps it was the responsibility of taking care of everything with family and all. She stops herself from thinking in this manner and decides to just go for the ride and really see what all of this is.

They take a motorboat over to the island, and she begins to get the real drift of what Robert's life has been like.

She tells herself, *Not bad. Except it looks like he has no routine of his own, only the life that seemed to be set up for him.* She felt like he had no real responsibilities.

Little did she know what she was about to embark on once they got to the island. They arrived at the dock, got off the boat, and began a rigorous tour around the town and visited his many businesses.

She had to regress on what she was thinking, as he had a lot of responsibility. He also had a way of living on the island, which was very laid-back and almost beautiful in its own way.

Robert suggested that since the sun was beginning to set that it would be great for her to experience one of his favorite restaurants.

They walked down a few blocks to a quaint restaurant that had a beautiful outdoor patio. He told Elaine that he wanted her to see this patio and enjoy the beautiful sunset that came almost every night there. It was mystical and amazing. As they arrive, all servants know him and exactly what he wants. Elaine figures that the restaurant must be owned by him, as they give him priority over everyone else.

They wine and dine together having a wonderful time. Elaine sips her wine and comments, "You really do have quite a few businesses here. All yours?"

Robert, takes a sip of his wine, and replies, "It sounds like you might be a little skeptical?"

Elaine takes a sip of her wine and looks over the glass at him. "Well, some of these businesses appear to be quite old. A little sarcastically, she says, "Were you eight years old when you first got these businesses?"

Robert frowns at her. "Well, I never thought about it. Are you trying to confuse me about my life?"

Elaine shakes her head. "No, guess I'm one of those overthinkers."

"Well, I can tell you this, I am incredibly happy with my life. How I got my businesses is really none of your business!"

Elaine looks down at the table with a bit of sadness creeping in. However, she cannot help but think that perhaps Robert will never remember her and the children or his prior life.

She looks up at Robert and acknowledges, "It certainly is beautiful here."

Robert senses and feels her sadness. "Please, don't let me make you sad. That's the last thing I want to do."

"Robert, what is it you would like to have come out of our meeting and spending time together?"

"You are such a sweetheart. I only want to get to know you better." I would like to learn how we met and what our life was like before the accident. You see, I had an accident and have been recovering for a while."

"If you really want to know, I can help you with that. I'm sure you will be very enlightened by what I have to tell you and show you."

Robert begins to get up and suggests that they go back to the house and have a nice long talk.

As she gets up, he grabs her arm and takes her hand, without hesitation. It was natural, like something he always did so many times before when they would walk together.

They walk hand in hand back to the boat, neither of them letting go of the others hand. Both hoping that by holding hands something great would happen. He smiles at her and says, "You really are one of the sweetest people I have ever known. She just smiles and keeps walking.

When they board the boat, Robert helps her and pulls her close smelling her hair once again. This catches Elaine by surprise; however, she does not pull away. She is entranced by his manner and how suave he is. Robert was trying to find some answers to the strange feeling he has whenever he is with her.

Chapter 27

Trusting the Truth

Renewal:

When they get back to the house, Robert goes up to his room and changes, and Elaine goes and get all the items she wants to show to Robert.

Robert joins Elaine on the veranda. Elaine is waiting sitting on a sofa with a box next to her. Robert sits down on the sofa with her.

"Are you ready?"

She begins to tell them how they had met when he was in his early twenties and spent many years as boyfriend and girlfriend.

Told him how even after they were married. They always courted each other.

She proceeds to tell him about where they lived in the city and how he worked so hard to get to where he was. She shows him a picture of the two of them getting married. He grabs the picture and stares at it. Making the statement out loud to himself, "We are married?"

"Yes, and we have been married for many years, at least thirteen years."

He grabs for the box. "I want to see it all."

She holds out the box, and he begins to look at many pictures of himself and Elaine. When he sees the pictures of the two little girls, he begins to cry. "Are they mine?"

She smiles. "Yes. Robert let's just not worry about you understanding all this right away. I want to talk about how I was brought to this island to meet you. I think this will help you. "Do you remember anything before being here on the island?"

He shakes his head, no.

"Robert let us just get out of the house and go sit on the beach and just talk. You don't have to grasp all of this at once."

Robert nods and stands up and says, "I need to do one thing first." He grabs her hands and pulls her to her feet and puts his arms around and just holds and gently sways side to side, smelling her hair and holding her close. He steps back and looks intensely at her. He tilts her chin up and looks into her eyes and kisses her long and tender on the lips.

She does not know whether to jump for joy or cry. She begins to weep and sees that Robert has tears running down his cheek, as well.

She smiles. "Looks like this is a lot for both of us."

"Yes. I want to know everything about my life, my children, and how all of this happened."

She looks at him as she begins to stand up and sighs. "It's a lot to know! I will have them brought to you tomorrow." They talk about the rest of the pictures in the box and how close he and the girls were.

"I would like to see the box that my father had Jama give to you."

Elaine says, "In the morning, let's meet in the kitchen and go through all of what is in the box."

Robert gets up and starts to walk inside the house; he looks back at her and says, "Let's look at it all tonight. I'll never be able to sleep. We started this; let's finish it. I need to know."

"Please don't get too upset; from what I see, it looks like you are coming out well and finding answers that you need to know."

Chapter 28

Resolution

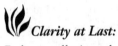 *Clarity at Last:*

Robert walks into the dining room and sits at the table. Elaine spreads all the documents out for him to begin to look at. Robert is amazed at how selfish his father really was.

"I never thought that my father would be so unfeeling for me and that he would keep my grandfather's will from me. However, guess I should have known, when he chose to send me to my grandparents every year and never seemed to spend any quality time with me."

As he is talking, Elaine is realizing that Robert's memory seems to be coming back very quickly.

"I don't even remember a birthday that he was with me. Not sure we even celebrated anything other than the words *happy birthday*. No, I'm not sure we even acknowledged that!?" Robert was getting angrier the more he talked. He looks at Elaine. "Do you know that he never, not even once, was willing to help me financially or otherwise! The amazing thing is that Patrick has now given up a major part of his wealth and signed it all over to me!"

Robert is shocked and has no idea how he will handle what has been given to him. However, he has decided that despite all the wealth his father has given him, that he has just ended any chance they had for a relationship.

Elaine held up her hand. "Robert, I need you to just listen to me for a bit. There is a lot that you need to know beyond all this paperwork. Robert, let's take a walk. I want to tell you some things you don't know. You need the whole picture."

They walk out of the house and head toward the beach. Robert takes a deep breath of the ocean air and says, "This is more relaxing already. I've always come down to the water to really seriously think."

Elaine, nods and smiles in agreement. They are walking along the shoreline as Elaine begins to talk. "Okay, now I will tell you what your father's attorney told me when he came here." She proceeded to tell Robert about how he had a concussion and they continued administering drugs to keep him in a state where he would only have short-term memory. She told him when she arrived that they stopped medicating him. She also told him about the auto accident and him being declared deceased. She also told him to know how she and her mom did everything they could with no luck in finding out what happened to him. "Robert, your daughters told me more than once how you would come to them and tell them to have me come and find you."

She told him about how Patrick came to her with the information on how to find him at the island. She also told him about Janet dying and how grieved Patrick was. She told him she felt her death and her wanting Patrick to settle things with Robert was a big turning point for Patrick. She told him how she felt that Janet was more the reason for all the greed than Patrick was. "I feel that her death has humbled him a lot."

Robert tells her that he is really interested in talking with Patrick about all of this.

"Think I'll call him in the morning to come home."

Chapter 29

Early Morning

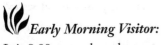 ***Early Morning Visitor:***

It is 8:00 a.m. when the screen door is opened, and Patrick walks through the door into the living room. Robert hears the door and walks into the living room from the hallway. When he sees Patrick, he lunges at him. His eyes turn dark and threating. He hits Patrick with both hands against the chest and knocks him onto the sofa.

Patrick is shocked and holds up his hands yelling, "Stop, just stop! I can explain everything!"

Robert yells at him, "Everything! Everything? I have just spent all night reading how my life is a lie and filled with deceit! You're telling me to hold it! I ought to knock you out!"

Elaine runs into the room with a look of shock! "Robert! Wait a moment!"

Robert turns and points to the hall. "Get out! This is between us!"

Elaine backs out into the hallway in complete shock. She has never seen Robert like this before.

Patrick says, "Your mother, Janet, is dead."

My mother? Don't you mean your wife!"

Patrick gets up and straightens himself around and sits down in the nearest chair. "Yes, my wife. She was a mother to you through your childhood."

Robert looks at him and softly says, "My mother… where is she?"

"She died when you were four years old. She was never really… healthy after she gave birth, and over the first few years, she just faded away.

"Oh my God, I had a real mother and you never told me! What is wrong with you?"

85

"You have lied to me all of my life and denied me any connection with people whom I may have loved. You deny me my real mother and then my grandparents, who were truly more parents to me than you ever could have been. As for you, you never even saw me or spent time with me. In fact, all of my school years you sent me off to schools that were away from you. I'm amazed that you have the gall to even say that you are sorry!"

Patrick just sits, looking down at the ground. "All I can say is that, now, I am deeply sorry."

Robert walks over closer to him and says, "Why couldn't you love me? Why did you hate me so much that you would try to take my life away from me?" Robert kind of chuckles and adds, "Destroying my childhood wasn't enough for you? So, you decided that you would just erase any memory or life that I may have had! Because of that you denied me a life and any connection with anyone that I could care for. You never spent time with me, so why was it so important?"

Patrick looks Robert in the face and quietly says, "The truth is I have always loved you. I was afraid to love and care about, I think, anyone after your mother died. I did not know what to do with a child or how to raise a child. I was lost for many years because I loved your mom so."

"So, what about dear, precious Janet?"

"Look, I had Janet appear in my life at a time that I really needed someone to be with me and for me. Janet was all that and more."

"Well, the more must not have been about taking any interest in me. I don't think I ever really did anything with her after I was in school, and I think I had a childcare person at the house before I went to school."

Patrick responds, a bit fed up with all of this. "Look, I married her in hopes she would be a good mother; however, she absolutely was not the mothering type. I needed her at that time more than you did. I loved her and married her, and I don't regret it for one minute. As far as hating you? I never did. I just did not know what to do with a child. I distanced myself from you because you reminded so much of your mother, and I could not let myself live in the loss of her."

Robert sighs. "That does not make everything okay."

"Just so you know, the reason all of this is out right now is because of Janet. Her dying wish was that I make everything right with you. By giving you everything in that box, it is my way of saying how sorry I am and that I truly want you to have a happy, good life."

Robert says, "I appreciate your honesty, but don't think I could ever trust you. All that you have given me does give me a brand-new life. I will be beginning and creating an entirely new life for me and all my family." Robert steps back from Patrick and says, "I could never and don't trust you completely with what you have done. I will take advantage of it. I cannot ever put my faith or trust in you. I will make sure all of this is in order."

Patrick nods, shakes his hand, "That is fine, son."

"Don't ever call me your son; as far as I'm concerned you do not exist!"

"That's okay; I've done everything I can to make amends." He turns and walks to the screen door, stops and looks Robert straight in the eyes and says, "Take care of yourself. You go ahead and do what you need to do. I will always see you as my son." He walks out the door, never looking back.

Chapter 30

A New Beginning

*Six Months Later:*

Robert comes out of the post office in town and heads straight for the beach where he knows he will find Elaine and the kids. He parks his car at home and kicks off his shoes and puts some swimming trunks on and heads for the beach.

Elaine and the kids are in sight. The kids happily playing in the water and Elaine is on a beach blanket. He thinks to himself, *This is the most happy and solid I have felt in a long time.* He smiles and sits down next to Elaine on the blanket and says, "I did it!"

They both, smile.

"I sent him a few million dollars and a couple of the downtown businesses; he should be fine for the rest of his life. "Don't really want him to worry at his age." They start to laugh together.

The kids are running ahead back to the house and Robert and Elaine are hand in hand and smiling. He looks at her and says, "This really is the good life."

As they enter the house, they hear Jama and Barbara, (Elaine's mom), in the kitchen laughing and talking.

Elaine smiles at Robert and says, "Wonder about those two. Wouldn't it be something if they became a couple?" She smiles, and Robert laughs.

Suddenly, the girls are calling to Robert, "Hurry, come here, a big package!"

Robert runs out the door and there is certainly a big box on the porch. He brings it in and sits in the big chair with the girls sitting together on a large footstool, looking into the box. Robert opens the package and pulls out an album of pictures. As he opens it, the first page is a photo of his birth mom and his father. They look so happy together he cannot believe his eyes. There are many pictures of Patrick and his mother, Lilly, together and smiling and even pictures at Christmas with him and a lot of things that they did with him as a baby before she died. Robert fights to hold back the tears.

"I really did have loving parents."

There is also a small diary of his mother's that tells how much she loved her husband and new baby... her death certificate and her birth certificate. There is also a note from Patrick that read: *I thought you deserved to know that you had two parents who loved you more than I can say.*

There was a picture that was taken at the funeral that had Patrick next to her coffin bowing down. A note from Patrick—*just wanted to let you know that your Mom and you meant everything to me. After she died, I lost all hope and did not know how to manage myself. Janet picked me up after your mother had been gone for about two years. She dusted me off and gave me a life. I always appreciated and loved her for that.*

My love for your mother will never have a match. I do love you. I just was afraid to love so intensely that I could not stand the thought of losing someone again. My distancing was the way I protected myself from having a broken heart.

Robert is shocked and wipes a tear away as he pulls out a large teddy bear with a tag that read: *First Christmas*

Robert does not know what to say or do. He tells the girls to be nice to the teddy bear that he is very special.

Robert looks at Elaine and asks, "How far away is Christmas?"

She says, "About four months."

He says, "Why don't we invite Grandpa! Elaine, we must always remember that family comes first, and love conquers all!"

They both hug and dance around in a circle with the girls.

Robert says, "I feel that I have been given a brand-new life that I love. It makes it so much easier when you forgive."

CPSIA information can be obtained
at www.ICGtesting.com
Printed in the USA
LVHW010402010821
694234LV00021B/1926